Gangsta Goat
and
The Big Moo

Written by
William Anthony

Illustrated by
Drue Rintoul

Can you say this sound and draw it with your finger?

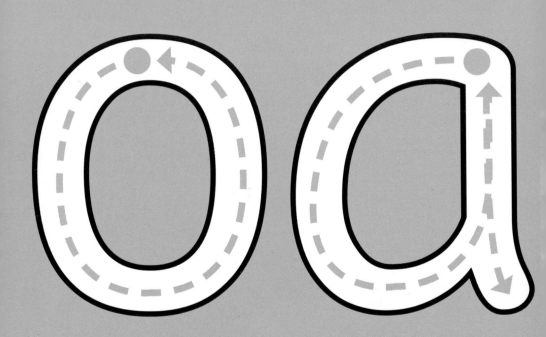

Gangsta Goat

Written by
William Anthony

Illustrated by
Drue Rintoul

Gaz is a goat.

But Gaz needs to be a gangsta goat.

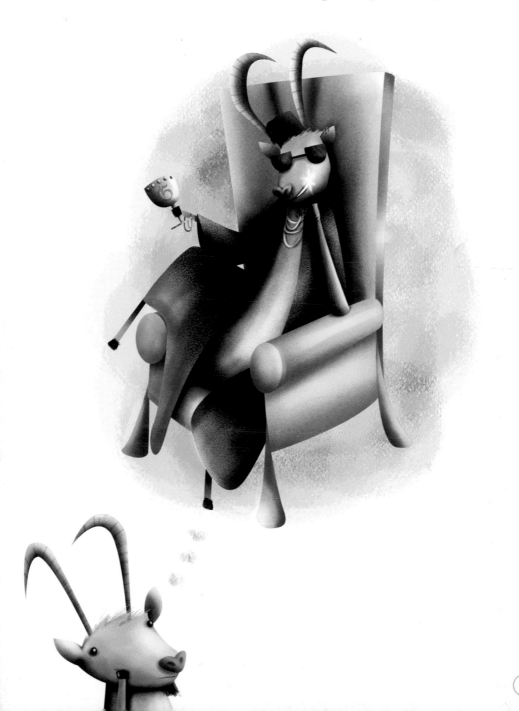

A gangsta goat needs a cool coat!

Gaz gets the coat full of fuzz.

Gaz looks good!

But he is not a gangsta yet.

A gangsta goat needs a cool boat!

Gaz hops off to the moat to get his boat.

He hops and bops on his boat.

But gangsta goats check boats for gaps.

But Gaz is not a gangsta. He is a...

... goat in a moat with a coat... but no boat.

Can you say this sound and draw it with your finger?

The Big Moo

Written by
William Anthony

Illustrated by
Drue Rintoul

"Moo at the Moon and it will fall," the fox tells Pam.

"It has got food, too!"

Pam is in shock, but she needs food.

The fox hops in the bush.
"MOO!" yells Pam.

The Moon will not fall. Pam will not get her food.

Pam needs a good plan.

She looks at books, but books are
no good.

"I need you all," she yells to the cows.

The cows look at the Moon and on
1... 2... 3...

The cows all yell a big "MOO!"
The Moon will not fall.

But a van with food is on the road.

The food rains on Pam, on the fox and on Gaz.

©2021 **BookLife Publishing Ltd.**
King's Lynn, Norfolk PE30 4LS

ISBN 978-1-83927-442-8
All rights reserved. Printed in Malaysia.
A catalogue record for this book is available from
the British Library.

Gangsta Goat & The Big Moo
Written by William Anthony
Illustrated by Drue Rintoul

An Introduction to BookLife Readers...

Our Readers have been specifically created in line with the London Institute of Education's approach to book banding and are phonetically decodable and ordered to support each phase of Letters and Sounds.

Each book has been created to provide the best possible reading and learning experience. Our aim is to share our love of books with children, providing both emerging readers and prolific page-turners with beautiful books that are guaranteed to provoke interest and learning, regardless of ability.

BOOK BAND GRADED using the Institute of Education's approach to levelling.

PHONETICALLY DECODABLE supporting each phase of Letters and Sounds.

EXERCISES AND QUESTIONS to offer reinforcement and to ascertain comprehension.

BEAUTIFULLY ILLUSTRATED to inspire and provoke engagement, providing a variety of styles for the reader to enjoy whilst reading through the series.

AUTHOR INSIGHT:
WILLIAM ANTHONY

Despite his young age, William Anthony's involvement with children's education is quite extensive. He has written over 60 titles with BookLife Publishing so far, across a wide range of subjects. William graduated from Cardiff University with a 1st Class BA (Hons) in Journalism, Media and Culture, creating an app and a TV series, among other things, during his time there.

William Anthony has also produced work for the Prince's Trust, a charity created by HRH The Prince of Wales that helps young people with their professional future. He has created animated videos for a children's education company that works closely with the charity.

PHASE 3
/oa/oo/ow/

This book focuses on the phonemes /oa/, /oo/ and /ow/ and is a yellow level 3 book band.